g A GOLDEN BOOK • NEW YORK

Tootle copyright © 1945, renewed 1973 by Random House LLC.
The Train to Timbuctoo copyright © 1951, renewed 1979 by Random House LLC.
The Little Red Caboose copyright © 1953, renewed 1981 by Marian Potter
and Random House LLC.

All rights reserved. This 2014 edition was published in the United States by
Golden Books, an imprint of Random House Children's Books, a division of
Random House LLC, a Penguin Random House Company, 1745 Broadway, New York,
NY 10019. The works that appear herein were originally published separately
by Simon and Schuster in 1945, 1951, and 1953. Golden Books, A Golden Book,
A Little Golden Book, the G colophon, and the distinctive gold spine are registered trademarks of
Random House LLC.
Visit us on the Web!
randomhouse.com/kids
Educators and librarians, for a variety of teaching tools, visit us at
RHTeachersLibrarians.com
Library of Congress Control Number: 2013947963
ISBN 978-0-385-37862-8
PRINTED IN CHINA
10 9 8 7 6 5 4

THE LITTLE RED
Caboose

By MARIAN POTTER
Illustrated by TIBOR GERGELY

FOR ANDREW, PAMELA, AND REBECCA

The little red caboose
always came last.

First came the big black engine,
puffing and chuffing.

Then came the boxcars,

then the oil cars,

then the coal cars,

then the flat cars.
Sometimes they were
switched around in different ways.

But the little red caboose
always came last.

Boys and girls waved at
the big black engine.

They listened to the boxcars
and the oil cars
and the coal cars
and the flat cars
go *clickety clack.*

But by the time the little red caboose
came along, the boys and girls were
turning away.

Because the little red caboose
always came last.

"Oh, smoke!" said the little red caboose.
"I wish I were a flat car
or a coal car or an oil car
or a boxcar, so boys and
girls would wave at me.

"How I wish I were a big black engine,
puffing and chuffing way up at the front
of the train!

"But I'm just the little old red caboose.
Nobody cares for me."

One day the train
started up a mountain.
Up went the big black engine.
Up went the boxcars.
Up went the oil cars.

Up went the coal cars.
Up went the flat cars.
Up went the little red caboose.

"Hang on tight, little caboose,"
called the flat car. "This is a
long tall mountain. And you
are the last car on the train."
"Don't I know it!"
sighed the little red caboose.
"Poor me!"

The train went slower
and slower and s-l-o-w-e-r.
Soon it was hardly moving.
It looked as if that train
could not get up the mountain.

"Look out, little caboose!"
called the flat car.
"The train is starting to slip
back down this long tall mountain!"
"Not if I can help it!"
said the little red caboose.

And he slammed on his brakes.
And he held tight to the tracks.
And he kept that train from
sliding down the mountain!

Then, *bump!*
The little red caboose
felt something push him
from behind.

It was two big black engines.
They pushed the train up to the top
of the mountain.

"We couldn't have done it,"
said the big black engines,
"if it had not been for the
little red caboose."
Everyone cheered.
And the little red caboose
nearly burst with pride.

Now, children wave at the big black engine and at all the cars.

But they save their biggest waves for the little red caboose. Because the little red caboose saved the train.

The Train to
TIMBUCTOO

By MARGARET WISE BROWN

Illustrated by ART SEIDEN

Clackety clack—clackety clack
There was a big train

and clickety click—clickety click—clickety click
There was a very little train.

They were on their way
home to Timbuctoo.
And they had just left
the town of Kalamazoo.

Slam Bang grease the engine
throw out the throttle and give it the gun.
There was a big engineer
who drove the big engine.

And Slam Bang grease the engine
throw out the throttle and give it the gun.
There was a little engineer
who drove the little engine.

When the big engine went through a tunnel
The big engineer blew his big whistle
whooooooooooooooooooooooooooooooo

When the little engine went through a tunnel
The little engineer blew his whistle
wheeeeeeeeeeeeeeeeeeeeeeeeeeeeeeeeeeeeeeeeeeeeeeeeee

And clackety clack—clickety click
Throw out the throttle and give it the gun
whoooooooooooooooooooooooooooooo
wheeeeeeeeeeeeeeeeeeeeeeeeeeeeeeeeeeeeeeeeeeeeeeeeeeeeeeee

Out from the big tunnel came the big engine
With the big engineer

And the big coal car

And the big baggage car

And the big passenger car

And the big dining car and the big

sleeping car and the little caboose

And then out from the little tunnel

Came the little engine
With the little engineer
And a little coal car

And the little baggage car

And the little passenger car

And the little dining car
And the little sleeping car
And a little caboose

Clickety click—clickety click
clackety clack—clackety clack
whoooooooooooooooooooooooooooooooooo
wheeeeeeeeeeeeeeeeeeeeeeeeeeeeeeeeeeeeeeeeeeeeeeeeeeeeeeeeeeeeeeeeee

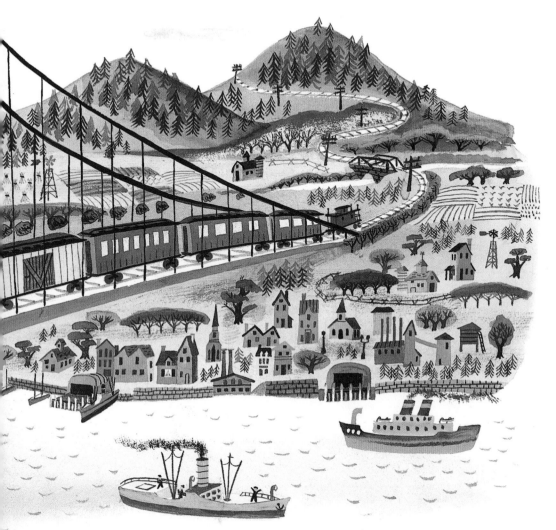

That great big train and that little tiny train
went roaring by.
Then clackety clack—clackety clack
The big train came to a big bridge
over a big river

And over the big bridge went the big engine

With
The big engineer
And the big coal car
And the big baggage car
And the big passenger car
And the big dining car
And the big sleeping car
And the little caboose

Then

Clickety click—clickety click

The little train came to a little bridge
Over a river, over a little river,

And clickety click—clickety click

Over the little bridge went the little engine

With the little engineer
And the little coal car
And the little baggage car
And the little passenger car
And the little dining car
And the little sleeping car
And the little caboose

And clickety click—clickety click
clackety clack—clackety clack—
pocketa—pocketa—pocketa—pocketa
picketa—picketa—picketa—picketa
The trains rolled on toward Timbuctoo
Far down the track from Kalamazoo
Until far away against the sky
There was a great big railroad station
And far away against the sky
There was a little railroad station.

whooooooooooo wheeeeeeeeeeeeeeeeee
As ringing their bells
dong—dong—dong ding—ding—ding
That great big train with a puff—puff—puff
And that tiny little train with a piff—piff—piff

Came home to Timbuctoo.

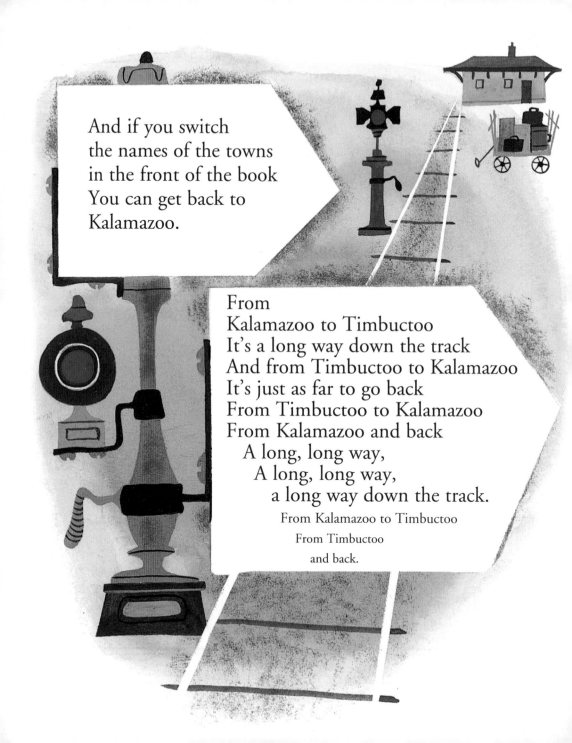

And if you switch
the names of the towns
in the front of the book
You can get back to
Kalamazoo.

From
Kalamazoo to Timbuctoo
It's a long way down the track
And from Timbuctoo to Kalamazoo
It's just as far to go back
From Timbuctoo to Kalamazoo
From Kalamazoo and back
A long, long way,
A long, long way,
a long way down the track.
From Kalamazoo to Timbuctoo
From Timbuctoo
and back.

TOOTLE

By GERTRUDE CRAMPTON

Illustrated by TIBOR GERGELY

Far, far to the west of everywhere is the village of
Lower Trainswitch. All the baby locomotives go there
to learn to be big locomotives. The young locomotives
steam up and down the tracks, trying to call out the
long, sad *ToooOoooot* of the big locomotives. But the
best they can do is a gay little *Tootle*.

Lower Trainswitch has a fine school for engines.
There are lessons in Whistle Blowing, Stopping for
a Red Flag Waving, Puffing Loudly When Starting,
Coming Around Curves Safely, Screeching When
Stopping, and Clicking and Clacking Over the Rails.

Of all the things that are taught in the Lower Trainswitch School for Locomotives, the most important is, of course, Staying on the Rails No Matter What.

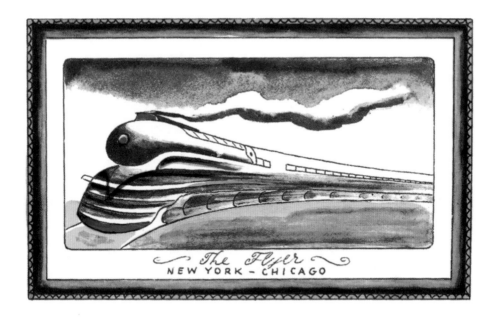

The Flyer
NEW YORK - CHICAGO

The head of the school is an old engineer named Bill. Bill always tells the new locomotives that he will not be angry if they sometimes spill the soup pulling the diner, or if they turn the milk to butter now and then. But they will never, never be good trains unless they get 100 A+ in Staying on the Rails No Matter What. All the baby engines work very hard to get 100 A+ in Staying on the Rails. After a few weeks not one of the engines in the Lower Trainswitch School for Trains would even think of getting off the rails, no matter—well, no matter what.

One day a new locomotive named Tootle came to school.

"Here is the finest baby I've seen since old 600," thought Bill. He patted the gleaming young locomotive and said, "How would you like to grow up to be the Flyer between New York and Chicago?"

"If a Flyer goes very fast, I should like to be one," Tootle answered. "I love to go fast. Watch me."

He raced all around the roundhouse.

"Good! Good!" said Bill. "You must study Whistle Blowing, Puffing Loudly When Starting, Stopping for a Red Flag Waving, and Pulling the Diner without Spilling the Soup.

"But most of all you must study Staying on the Rails No Matter What. Remember, you can't be a Flyer unless you get 100 A+ in Staying on the Rails."

Tootle promised that he would remember and that he would work very hard.

He did, too.

He even worked hard at Stopping for a Red Flag Waving. Tootle did not like those lessons at all. There is nothing a locomotive hates more than stopping.

But Bill said that no locomotive ever, ever kept going when he saw a red flag waving.

One day, while Tootle was practicing for his lesson in Staying on the Rails No Matter What, a dreadful thing happened.

He looked across the meadow he was running through and saw a fine, strong black horse.

"Race you to the river," shouted the black horse, and kicked up his heels.

Away went the horse. His black tail streamed out behind him, and his mane tossed in the wind. Oh, how he could run!

"Here I go," said Tootle to himself.

"If I am going to be a Flyer, I can't let a horse beat me," he puffed. "Everyone at school will laugh at me."

His wheels turned so fast that they were silver streaks. The cars lurched and bumped together. And just as Tootle was sure he could win, the tracks made a great curve.

"Oh, Whistle!" cried Tootle. "That horse will beat me now. He'll run straight while I take the Great Curve."

Then the Dreadful Thing happened. After all that Bill had said about Staying on the Rails No Matter What, Tootle jumped off the tracks and raced alongside the black horse!

The race ended in a tie. Both Tootle and the black horse were happy. They stood on the bank of the river and talked.

"It's nice here in the meadow," Tootle said.

When Tootle got back to school, he said nothing about leaving the rails. But he thought about it that night in the roundhouse.

"Tomorrow I will work hard," decided Tootle. "I will not even think of leaving the rails, no matter what."

And he did work hard. He practiced tootling so much that the Mayor Himself ran up the hill, his green coattails flapping, and said that everyone in the village had a headache and would he please stop TOOTLING.

So Tootle was sent to practice Staying on the Rails No Matter What.

As he came to the Great Curve, Tootle looked across the meadow. It was full of buttercups.

"It's like a big yellow carpet. How I should like to play in them and hold one under my searchlight to see if I like butter!" thought Tootle. "But no, I am going to be a Flyer and I must practice Staying on the Rails No Matter What!"

Tootle clicked and clacked around the Great Curve. His wheels began to say over and over again, "Do you like butter? Do you?"

"I don't know," said Tootle crossly. "But I'm going to find out."

He stopped much faster than any good Flyer ever does, unless he is stopping for a Red Flag Waving. He hopped off the tracks and bumped along the meadow to the yellow buttercups.

"What fun!" said Tootle.

And he danced around and around and held one of the buttercups under his searchlight.

"I do like butter!" cried Tootle. "I do!"

At last the sun began to go down, and it was time to hurry to the roundhouse.

That evening while the Chief Oiler was playing checkers with old Bill, he said, "It's queer. It's very queer, but I found grass between Tootle's front wheels today."

"Hmm," said Bill. "There must be grass growing on the tracks."

"Not on our tracks," said the Day Watchman, who spent his days watching the tracks and his nights watching Bill and the Chief Oiler play checkers.

Bill's face was stern. "Tootle knows he must get 100 A+ in Staying on the Rails No Matter What, if he is going to be a Flyer."

Next day Tootle played all day in the meadow.
He watched a green frog and he made a daisy chain.
He found a rain barrel, and he said softly, "Toot!"
"TOOT!" shouted the barrel. "Why, I sound like
a Flyer already!" cried Tootle.

That night the First Assistant Oiler said he had found a daisy in Tootle's bell. The day after that, the Second Assistant Oiler said that he had found hollyhock flowers floating in Tootle's eight bowls of soup.

And then the Mayor Himself said that he had seen Tootle chasing butterflies in the meadow. The Mayor Himself said that Tootle had looked very silly, too.

Early one morning Bill had a long, long talk with the Mayor Himself.

When the Mayor Himself left the Lower Trainswitch School for Locomotives, he laughed all the way to the village.

"Bill's plan will surely put Tootle back on the track," he chuckled.

Bill ran from one store to the next, buying ten yards of this and twenty yards of that and all you have of the other. The Chief Oiler and the First, Second, and Third Assistant Oilers were hammering and sawing instead of oiling and polishing. And Tootle? Well, Tootle was in the meadow watching the butterflies flying and wishing he could dip and soar as they did.

Not a store in Lower Trainswitch was open the next day and not a person was at home. By the time the sun came up, every villager was hiding in the meadow along the tracks. And each of them had a red flag. It had taken all the red goods in Lower Trainswitch, and hard work by the Oilers, but there was a red flag for everyone.

Soon Tootle came tootling happily down the tracks. When he came to the meadow, he hopped off the tracks and rolled along the grass. Just as he was thinking what a beautiful day it was, a red flag poked up from the grass and waved hard. Tootle stopped, for every locomotive knows he must Stop for a Red Flag Waving.

"I'll go another way," said Tootle.

He turned to the left, and up came another waving red flag, this time from the middle of the buttercups.

When he went to the right, there was another red flag waving.

There were red flags waving from the buttercups, in the daisies, under the trees, near the bluebirds' nest, and even one behind the rain barrel. And, of course, Tootle had to stop for each one, for a locomotive must always Stop for a Red Flag Waving.

"Red flags," muttered Tootle. "This meadow is full of red flags. How can I have any fun?

"Whenever I start, I have to stop. Why did I think this meadow was such a fine place? Why don't I ever see a green flag?"

Just as the tears were ready to slide out of his boiler, Tootle happened to look back over his coal car. On the tracks stood Bill, and in his hand was a big green flag. "Oh!" said Tootle.

He puffed up to Bill and stopped.

"This is the place for me," said Tootle. "There is nothing but red flags for locomotives that get off their tracks."

"Hurray!" shouted the people of Lower Trainswitch, and jumped up from their hiding places. "Hurray for Tootle the Flyer!"

Now Tootle is a famous Two-Miles-a-Minute Flyer. The young locomotives listen to his advice.

"Work hard," he tells them. "Always remember to Stop for a Red Flag Waving. But most of all, Stay on the Rails No Matter What."